This
Faber book
belongs to:

FABER & FABER has published children's books since 1929. Some of our very first publications included *Old Possum's Book of Practical Cats* by T. S. Eliot starring the now world-famous Macavity, and *The Iron Man* by Ted Hughes. Our catalogue at the time said that 'it is by reading such books that children learn the difference between the shoddy and the genuine'. We still believe in the power of reading to transform children's lives.

→ A FABER PICTURE BOOK ←

Mungojerrie and Rumpelteazer

Written by T. S. Eliot

Illustrated by Arthur Robins

ff

FABER & FABER

Mungojerrie and Rumpelteazer were a very
notorious couple of cats.
As knockabout clowns, quick-change comedians,
tight-rope walkers and acrobats

They had an extensive reputation.
They made their home in Victoria Grove—

That was merely their centre of operation,
for they were incurably given to rove.

They were very well known
in Cornwall Gardens, in Launceston Place,
and in Kensington Square—

They had really a little more reputation
than a couple of cats can very well bear.

If the area window
was found ajar

And the basement
looked like a
field of war,

If a tile or two came
loose on the roof,

Which presently ceased to be waterproof,

If the drawers were pulled out from
the bedroom chests,

And you couldn't
find one
of your
winter vests,

Or after supper one of the girls

Suddenly missed her Woolworth pearls:

Then the family would say:
'It's that horrible cat!

It was Mungojerrie—or Rumpelteazer!'—
And most of the time they left it at that.

Mungojerrie and Rumpelteazer had a very unusual gift of the gab.

They were highly efficient cat-burglars as well,

and remarkably smart at a smash-and-grab.

They made their home in Victoria Grove. They had no regular occupation.

They were plausible fellows, and liked to engage a friendly policeman in conversation.

When the family assembled for Sunday dinner,
With their minds made up that they wouldn't
get thinner

On Argentine joint, potatoes and greens,

And the cook would appear from
behind the scenes

And say in a voice that was broken
  with sorrow:
'I'm afraid you must wait
  and have dinner tomorrow!
For the joint has gone
  from the oven—
    like that!'

Then the family would say:
'It's that horrible cat!

It was Mungojerrie—or Rumpelteazer!'—
And most of the time they left it at that.

Mungojerrie and Rumpelteazer had a wonderful way of working together.

And some of the time you
would say it was luck,

and some of the time you
would say it was weather.

They would go through
the house
like a hurricane,

and no sober
person could
take his
oath

Was it Mungojerrie—or Rumpelteazer?

or could you have sworn that it mightn't be both?

And when you heard a dining-room **smash**

Or up from the pantry there came a loud **crash**

Or down from the library came a loud _ping_
From a vase which was commonly said to be Ming—

Then the family would say:
'Now which was which cat?

It was Mungojerrie! AND Rumpelteazer!'—
And there's nothing at all to be done about that!

From the original collection,
'respectfully dedicated to those friends who have assisted its
composition by their encouragement, criticism and suggestions:
and in particular to Mr T. E. Faber, Miss Alison Tandy,
Miss Susan Wolcott, Miss Susanna Morley, and the Man in White Spats. O.P.'

First published in 1939 in Old Possum's Book of Practical Cats
by Faber and Faber Ltd,
Bloomsbury House, 74—77 Great Russell Street, London WC1B 3DA
This edition first published in the UK in 2018
This edition first published in the US in 2018

Printed in Malta

A CIP record for this book is available from the British Library
ISBN 978—0—571—32486—6

2 4 6 8 10 9 7 5 3